MW00563564

THE GROTESQUE CHILD

THE GROTESQUE CHILD

a novel by

KIM PARKO

TARPAULIN SKY PRESS
CA ∴ CO ∴ NY ∴ VT
2016

The Grotesque Child
© 2016 Kim Parko
ISBN-13: 978-1-939460-05-9
Printed and bound in the USA

Cover art by the author.

Sections from this manuscript previously appeared in the journals
Tarpaulin Sky and *Yeti*.

Tarpaulin Sky Press
P.O. Box 189
Grafton, Vermont 05146
www.tarpaulinsky.com

For more information on Tarpaulin Sky Press trade paperback
and hand-bound editions, as well as information regarding distribution, personal orders, and catalogue requests, please visit our
website at tarpaulinsky.com.

to Rowan

PART I

The mother ship could not bring a child to term. She searched the worlds for someone to help her with her problem. In one of the worlds, she found the midwife, Brigit, who was purported to make the most barren wombs fertile. Brigit moved onto the mother ship and stayed in a room on the edge of the mother ship's goop chamber. The goop chamber was where the mother ship's children should have spawned. Brigit threw herbs into the goop. She squirted tinctures into the goop. She chanted over the goop with burning incense. She advised the mother ship about exercises, diet and stress reduction, and the mother ship followed her advice diligently. The mother ship had also prayed, nightly, to no-one-in-particular. But all the mother ship's children came out too early, too small, and barely formed. She had watched them all eject through her birthing hole and float away from her as bloody clumps without the fins to swim.

What kind of mother ship am I? cried the mother ship to Brigit. One that cannot bear children? Who has ever heard of such a travesty?

Brigit tried to comfort the mother ship, but Brigit knew that what the mother ship really needed was new seeds.

Brigit had given her own seeds away long ago.

One night the mother ship asked no-one-in-particular, Can you tell me whether or not I should have children? And if not, could you rename me as something other than the mother ship, and if I should have children, can you help me know what I should do to bear them? And the mother ship tried to interpret no-one-in-particular's silence.

The mother ship then asked the same question to Brigit, who then took out the colorful array of cards that she always carried with her. Brigit spread the cards on a table and carefully discerned their message.

It's clear, the midwife said to the mother ship, the cards say that you must find the grotesque child.

***

The grotesque child had been in the dark cavern a long time. She longed for something she could not envision, having never seen light. The grotesque child began to eat her way out of the cavern. After many days of eating, she bit through to light. The light daggered into her eye pits, leaving her disoriented. Was it wrong for me to want this? she asked no-one-in-particular.

Then she said to no-one-in-particular, Where am I?

It was too bright for the grotesque child to see in the daylight, so she explored her surroundings at night. Also, the wind blew fiercely in the day, but subsided to a gentle breeze by twilight. The grotesque child wandered the land under the stars and moon, and when the moon disappeared, she touched everything with her feelers, and listened to every sound with her large ears, and smelled all around her with her quivering nose, and thus, the grotesque child began to know the world that she had eaten her way into.

***

The animal was nocturnal. In the day, the animal curled itself beneath a boulder. The animal called the boulder mother, but the boulder did not feed the animal. The animal remembered that its real mother had fed it milk from a ring of teats that surrounded the real mother's heart. The animal always thought, Did I drain my real mother's heart? Is that why she's gone?

The animal and the grotesque child were both in search of food during a night when the moon had roamed from the sky. The grotesque child thought that the moon, too, had gone in search of food, for she could never tell what the moon might eat up there in the sky devoid of all but stars. She imagined a sky that existed beyond this sky, a sky that filled with delectable orbs, and she imagined the moon pulling the orbs into its crater and savoring them.

The animal and the grotesque child were touching, listening, smelling and tasting. They were discerning what was meant to be eaten and what was meant to be left alone. When they came upon one another, and after they had touched and listened and smelled and tasted each other, they could not discern what each other were. So the grotesque child said to the animal, Who are you?

I don't know who I am, said the animal, my mother never got a chance to tell me. Who are you?

I don't know who I am either, said the grotesque child. And she asked, What is a mother?

A mother is who you came out of, said the animal.

I ate my way out of a cavern where I had been for a very long time, said the grotesque child. I got tired of being there and I eventually bit my way into this place. But at times, this place is too bright for me and the wind is too harsh against my skin.

Yes, said the animal, I feel the same way about this place. In the day, I curl up under a boulder that I call mother. My new mother protects me, but she can't feed me like my real mother did.

After that moonless night, the two were inseparable. They slept under the boulder-mother together. They went out at night together, sensing together what they could eat. It went on like this for many years.

***

The grotesque child was under the boulder with the animal. She was listening to the wind. She thought, I would really like to go out into the day. I want to see what the food I've been eating looks like. She told the animal, I'm going to go out into the day and I'm going to tell the wind to calm down. The animal said, Be careful; the wind can be tricky.

The grotesque child emerged from under the boulder. She shielded her eyes from the brightness. She encountered the wind immediately.

Could you please calm down? she asked the wind.

Only if you let me enter you, said the wind.

What will you do once inside me? she asked.

I will course through your wind-channels.

And if I let you enter me and course through my wind-channels, you promise that you'll calm down?

Oh, yes. I promise.

The wind said, Are you ready?

The grotesque child opened her mouth and let the wind enter. The wind thrashed around in her convoluted viscera. The grotesque child was wind-sick.

The wind said, Grotesque child, there is not one clear passageway through you.

Outside, the wind had calmed down, but inside it poked, prodded, and distorted the grotesque child. The animal emerged from the boulder, shielding its eyes. It saw the grotesque child for the first time. The child is distorted, thought the animal. The grotesque child was thrashing wildly on the ground. What is wrong? asked the animal. I'm wind-sick, said the grotesque child, the wind said that there is not one clear passageway through me.

The animal looked into the grotesque child's eyes and saw that they were cloudy. It looked at her tongue and saw that it was coated in white film. It pressed into her abdomen and felt that her coiled channels were blocked by hobgoblins.

The animal made multiple incisions in the grotesque child's stomach with its teeth and sucked the hobgoblins from her channels. The grotesque child watched as the animal sucked out each hobgoblin and spit it into a bowl. The animal put needles into the hobgoblins' feet. They groaned and writhed and turned to moths. When the animal had a bowl of moths, it said to the grotesque child, Drink. It tilted her head back and she drank the moths.

The wind carried the moths through her cleared-out channels. The moths settled in each of her organs and quietly fluttered.

Now the wind had calmed during the day, but the brightness was too much for the grotesque child's and the animal's eyes. Both the grotesque child and the animal had huge eyes. They walked around shielding their huge eyes from the brightness; nevertheless, they both developed debilitating headaches. I am going to ask the brightness to dim down a bit, said the animal to the grotesque child. Be careful, said the grotesque child, the brightness can be tricky.

The animal emerged from under the boulder into the brightness, shielding its eyes as it emerged. The animal asked the brightness, Do you think you could dim down a bit? The brightness said to the animal, Only if you let me enter you. What will you do once inside me? asked the animal. I will illuminate your dark recesses, said the brightness.

The animal opened its mouth and let the brightness enter. The brightness said, You have so many recesses. As the brightness entered each recess, the animal moaned.

The grotesque child heard the moaning and went out into the brightness that was now dim enough that she did not need to shield her eyes. She saw the animal moaning and asked, What is wrong? The brightness has entered me and has exposed all that is hidden in my darkest recesses, said the animal. I am afraid of what has come to light inside me.

The grotesque child went out that night and gathered seeds from the night-food they had been eating. She fed them to the animal. The next day and the animal felt relief as the seeds bloomed and covered its recesses in partial shade.

Now that the wind had calmed and the brightness had dimmed, the grotesque child and the animal were free to roam the land in the day.

The day-land was so different from the night-land and they felt some of their night-land-senses atrophying while their day-land-eyes got bigger and wider.

The grotesque child and the animal roamed far and wide in the day and they became sleepy at night. Soon they were only eating day food.

One day, as they roamed, they spotted something in the distance. It was massive with gleaming scales and a spine that jutted into the air. Is it alive? asked the grotesque child. The grotesque child and the animal watched the gleaming, jutting mass for hours, but it did not move. Whatever that is, said the animal, I think we should stay well away from it.

It was dark and the grotesque child and the animal were sleeping under the boulder-mother. They were awoken by bright lights and strange voices. They did not have time to react before they were put in a container from which they could not escape. It was dark in the container, darker than any moonless night. They were both afraid.

Quick, said the grotesque child to the animal, hide in one of my nooks. The animal climbed deep into one of the grotesque child's nooks and hid there.

When the captors opened the container, they were confused. They thought they had captured two creatures: one furry and soft and one distorted. But now there was only one: the grotesque one. Even though it's grotesque, it's only a child, said one of the captors. One can learn a lot about the mechanisms of sensitivity and desensitization from a child, said the other captor.

The grotesque child and the animal were brought into the middle of the gleaming mass and to the top of one of its jutting spines.

The grotesque child was able to survive because the animal remained hidden within her nook. When the pain was at its worst, the animal sang lullabies within her, soothing her exposed nerves and spasming muscles. When the captors left, the animal came out of the grotesque child's nook and licked her wounds. The captors were amazed at the grotesque child's resiliency.

After weeks of vivisection, one of the captors said, This child has been through enough.

The other captor said, We are just beginning.

One of the captors was a doctor by day and a healer by night. The doctor thought, Could this experimentation lead us to a greater capacity to understand suffering? The healer thought, I can't bear to witness any more suffering.

The other captor was of elusive profession. And of unquestionable authority.

The captor of unquestionable authority was instructing the doctor to remove the outer sheath of the grotesque child's feelers. Without the sheaths the feelers would interpret the most minuscule of stimuli as pain.

The captor of unquestionable authority amused himself by blowing gently over the grotesque child and watching her writhe.

When the doctor stood over the writhing child, he could feel an invisible force coming from the child's feelers. He felt the force penetrate through his outer and middle layers. He felt the force wrap itself around the healer trapped in his core. The force pulled at the healer. He felt the healer emerging, while the doctor sank into his hollowed-out core.

As the healer was emerging and the doctor was sinking, the doctor poked one of the healer's eyes into his head and screeched into the healer's ear.

When the healer emerged, he had an inward eye and an outward eye, a hearing ear and a deaf one.

The healer wrapped the grotesque child in the softest cloth he could find, but still the touch of fabric to her feelers was unbearable. Inside her nook, the animal hummed.

The healer took the grotesque child to his village cottage and placed her on a mat. He went to his cabinet in search of a soothing balm, but he could find nothing that would protect the feelers from the relentless pain of even the air.

The healer thought and thought and as he was thinking, the animal crawled out of the grotesque child's nook. The healer was surprised to see the animal. We thought you had escaped, he said.

I have learned a great deal about the grotesque child by hiding in her nook, said the animal. I think that water is the only thing that will soothe her.

The healer filled his large caldron with water and lifted the grotesque child off the matt and gently submerged her. Her writhing and spasming and moaning immediately stopped, and within minutes, she began to swim.

***

The mother ship searched the worlds for the grotesque child. She searched the dead worlds and the dying worlds. She searched the just born worlds and the worlds that were in the prime of life. In every world she pulled a child into her hull, hoping it was the grotesque child. But the children she abducted were not grotesque; each child was frightened and unloving toward the mother ship, and she ended up expelling each one, lifeless, back onto it's world.

The mother ship hovered over the village. The villagers told the healer that the mother ship came every year. There was no stopping her. They told the healer, We've tried to catch her with our sky-nets, but to no avail. When the mother ship came, she took a child back with her into space.

The healer thought of the grotesque child: the motherless child. He thought of her wide eyes that looked like they were taking in more than sight, and her feelers that extended out of her like animal whiskers. They were highly sensitive, so much so that she could only be out of the caldron for a few minutes before her nervous system became overwhelmed, incapacitated.

The grotesque child had always wanted to come out and play with the other village children. The healer had thought, If only I could remove the feelers. He tried slicing one off once, a, quick, painless chop from the cleaver. Or so he thought. The grotesque child's scream was intolerable, and the absent feeler sprouted scar tissue that still flinched at the touch of air.

When the mother ship came, she sang a mournful song in the sky.

The grotesque child was in the caldron. She floated in dark water. Her feelers were limp, her wide eyes shut. The mother ship's song echoed through the water and into the grotesque child's ears.

The grotesque child told the animal, My mother is calling me.

When the mother ship met the atmosphere, a thundering fountain spewed through her blowhole. The thunder reverberated around the village. All the children hid as the deluge fell.

The animal told the healer that the grotesque child wished to go to the mother ship.

The healer thought, The mother ship is looking for nothing so strange. All she wants is a child to love her back, not like all the children who have come with her kicking and screaming and then, once in the depths of space, so cold and still. All she wants is a child to cradle in her hull and to soothe to sleep within the stars.

The healer and the animal wheeled the caldron below the mother ship and beckoned her. The mother ship sent down a long tube and sucked up the caldron and the animal and the healer into her hull.

When the mother ship saw the grotesque child in the enormous caldron, she was doubtful. The mother ship asked the healer and the animal, What am I to do with a child in a caldron? The animal said, All she needs is a place to swim. Well then, said the mother ship, she can swim in my goop.

The healer and the animal wheeled the grotesque child's caldron to the edge of the mother ship's goop. They tipped the caldron and the grotesque child slipped easily into the mother ship's goop.

The grotesque child spent most of her time swimming in the mother ship's goop. Each time she emerged from the goop, her feelers were coated with a film that dulled their sensitivity. The grotesque child was able to leave the mother ship's goop and limp through the halls of the mother ship with little pain.

Brigit watched the grotesque child swimming in the mother ship's goop. The grotesque child is at home in the goop, thought Brigit. But now that the grotesque child has come on board, the mother ship still does not conceive children.

Brigit asked the grotesque child, Have you carried anything with you? The grotesque child thought only of the animal. But is there anything else you've brought with you? asked Brigit. The grotesque child checked all her nooks and crannies. Deep within a cranny she found a handful of night-land seeds that she had used to help cast shade over the animal's internal brightness. The grotesque child showed the seeds to Brigit. Brigit looked closely at the seeds. She thought, These are the seeds the mother ship needs. Brigit said, The next time you swim, could you disperse these seeds in the mother ship's goop?

Within the mother ship's goop, the night-land seeds sprouted, and then turned embryonic and then turned fetal.

***

How did you become a midwife?

My generation had empty wombs. No one knew why we all had empty wombs. And try as we might to fill them, we went to bed each night and could feel the wind howling through our wombs.

We were punished by the older generations, for whose fault could it be than our own? The older generations believed that we had willed our empty wombs: that we had made a pact amongst ourselves and that we ate a secret herb that burned the contents of our womb as a fire burns a forest.

Our punishment was confinement with scheduled visits from the men of our generation. While in confinement, I put my ear to one empty womb and then another. I heard the stories of the wombs as told by the howling wind.

The empty-womb stories were all the same: they were not empty. Each womb had three tiny seeds that refused to bloom.

I consulted my colorful array of cards. I didn't know where the cards had come from, but they had been with me since my first memory. My memory was of reaching down into a pocket in the skin of my belly and finding them there. When I pulled out the cards, the pocket in the skin of my belly vanished.

I spread the cards on the table and carefully deciphered their message. The cards said that our water source caused the reluctance in our wombs. We drew our water from a sour river that ran alongside our village.

Late that night, I reached into my own womb. My fingers felt the nuances of the space inside until they came upon the three tiny seeds. How could I feel them? They were tinier than grains of sand. It was this gift of feeling what others couldn't that separated me.

I held my seeds in a tight fist and I left the confinement cottage. The other women were afraid for me, but they were also hoping that I would find the reason for our dormant wombs.

I was in search of the source of the souring river. The older generations spoke of a sweet and clear river that our generation had never known. I walked one way as the river flowed the other. Eventually I saw in the distance a shiny, jutting beast in the river. As I came closer, I saw it squatting in the river. A sour yellow stream flowed from between its haunches.

I came up to the beast and asked, Why are you defiling the river?

I like to cool my haunches in the river, and I like to watch my sour yellowness mix and mingle with the clearness and flow down the river, said the beast in a vacant tone.

Where do you come from?

I was made by the children who renounced their mother.

And now you defile the river without thought?

It is not that so much as that I enjoy cooling myself here and I enjoy pissing here.

Do you have children yourself?

Oh yes, you should see them.

Where are they?

The beast reached into its pouch and pulled out three tiny embryos, dead and covered in mold.

It was then that I loosened my mind and floated it over to the beast's mind. My mind enveloped the beast's mind, conforming to it contours. My mind was so disoriented by the contours of the beast's mind that I found myself dizzy and vomiting. When my mind disengaged from the beast's mind and floated back to me, I knew that the twisted contours of the beast's mind meant that it was suffering.

I traveled back to the confinement cottage and snuck in. I told the women, there is a beast upriver, and as long as it suffers, so will we.

I began to sneak out and visit the beast daily. I wondered about the children who made this beast. Why would they renounce their mother? Why would they make this beast that could only sit in the river defiling it?

Where are the children who made you? I asked the beast.

They are inside me, said the beast.

What do you mean?

The beast said nothing, but it rolled down its long tongue. I stepped onto its tongue, grasping the rails on either side. I began the ascent to the threshold of the beast's mouth.

I arrived to the lip of the beast's mouth and I looked inside. The inside of the beast was lit with a too-bright light. It disoriented me. When my eyes adjusted, I saw gleaming cubes connected to straight lines. I saw the children moving frenetically across the lines from cube to cube. What is in those cubes? I asked myself.

I climbed down the throat of the beast to find out.

The cubes were filled with flat, moving images that had no taste or texture or smell. They were vividly colored and they hummed. The children stared agape at the images. When the images stopped moving, the children ran quickly on to the next cube.

The children seemed to be enchanted by these images, and the brightness and frenzy of their movements made the inside of the beast unbearably hot. No wonder the beast's own children can't survive, I thought. And no wonder the beast has to cool its haunches in the river.

I thought, There must be a central power source to all this brightness and frenzy. I walked for days through the cubes until I came to a central power plant that emitted a penetrating buzz that agitated my blood.

Within the central power plant I found a lever.

I simply pulled it down and the beast went dark.

There was great commotion in the beast as the children tried to orient themselves in the blackness. In the distance a small circle of light could be seen. The children thrust their way toward it. There were screams as the children trampled each other to escape through the small circle of light. The small circle of light was the beast's mouth opening out into an unknown world.

After the children left, I hid for years in the cool darkness of the beast. I watched as the cubes began to disintegrate from disuse. Weed roots cracked their foundations. Vines ate their sides. Leaves fell to the hard floors, mixed with the dead bodies of the trampled children, and rotted in layers. Worms ingested decay and excreted dark, rich nutrients. The beast's embryos burrowed in the humus. They turned fetal. Then the beast gave birth.

The babies were born unmoving. Again. As I stood over the unmoving forms, my seeds twitched in my hand. Their movement told me something I didn't want to know: if I fed each of the babies one of my seeds, they would move. I knew this also: These were the only seeds I would ever have; without them, I would never give birth.

I fed the babies my seeds. The babies began to squirm. They began to cry. The beast rose from the river. It moved into the forest to suckle its babies. The soured river ran clear again.

PART II

***

The healer now lives in a crook of the mother ship and they converse through a vent that leads to a duct that leads to the middle chamber that holds the mother ship's goop. The mother ship's goop is an amalgamation of every body fluid. From the mother ship's goop, the new children rise.

The grotesque child swims, daily, in the mother ship's goop.

The mothers ship says to the healer, The grotesque child is perfectly balanced in my goop. How can we make her perfectly balanced out of my goop?

The healer says, Maybe we should separate your goop into each of its individual body fluids and administer these to the grotesque child in the form of small, round pellets that can dissolve under her tongue.

The goop is a mess. It is viscous in some places, creamy in others, runny elsewhere. It is pungent and bitter. It is salty and metallic and sweet and vile. It burns and soothes. The healer unfurls his long tongue and begins the task of distinguishing. When the healer has separated all the mother ship's body fluids, he forms them into small, round pellets.

Look how balanced you are since you started taking the small, round pellets, the mother ship says to the grotesque child.

Have you noticed that since we separated your goop, there is nothing for the new children to rise out of ? says the grotesque child.

Yes, I've noticed, but now that you are balanced, do we really need new children?

The grotesque child walks in a smooth, upright gait down the halls of the mother ship. Her arms sway in rhythm. Her head is no longer cocked to the side. Her painful cysts have abated, leaving immaculate pores.

The grotesque child walks the halls of the mother ship all day and night and does not tire, but she longs for her daily swim in the mother ship's goop.

Brigit says, I notice that there is no more goop for the new children to rise out of.

It's true, says the mother ship, but have you seen the grotesque child? She is no longer grotesque.

I have seen the grotesque child and it's true she is more balanced and upright and that she moves with rhythm, but she is no longer sleeping and making her dreams.

I do miss her dreams, says the mother ship sadly.

Without the grotesque child's dreams and the new children rising out of the goop, what is our mission?

The mother ship has no answer.

The children that rose from the mother ship's goop after the night seeds were planted have matured. In their pods, they disperse from the mother mother ship in all directions. The mother ship misses her children. But I have the grotesque child, thinks the mother ship. And she is comforted.

The grotesque child continues to wander the halls of the mother ship throughout the night and day.

The mother ship asks the grotesque child how she's feeling. The grotesque child says, I am feeling the hole deepening and widening. I am feeling that the pests eradicated indiscriminately from the dead worlds that were once alive are constructing vessels in the eradication sphere. I am feeling bear-steps climbing the footholds. I am feeling the solidification of a dense, dark orb in my center.

The mother ship retreats to her pillow space-cloud of soft debris. It is the only place she can think clearly. The mother ship thinks for many days. She makes a decision.

The mother ship asks the healer to take the small round pellets and reconstitute them back into her goop.

The healer reaches down the grotesque child's throat and pulls out a dense, dark orb. He places the dark orb in a cauldron and melts it back to the mother ship's goop.

The mother ship's goop is reconstituted by the healer, but the grotesque child can't swim in the reconstituted goop. When she goes into the deep end of the goop, she barely makes it back to the shallows. The grotesque child says to the mother ship, Your reconstituted goop is yucky.

The grotesque child has lost her outward seeing eyes and the mother ship is growing dead children from her goop.

The mother ship contacts the healer and says to him, The grotesque child won't go near the goop. She cannot swim in it without sinking. It fills her mouth and she wants to gag. And the new children rising up out of it are rising up dead.

The healer inspects the mother ship's goop. The goop is different. It has lost a bitter quality that it once possessed. It is too sweet and fragrant.

The healer tastes the goop with his long tongue, carefully distinguishing the one thousand twelve component bodily fluids. After many days, he tells the mother ship that she is missing her bile.

Where has my bile gone? the mother ship asks no-one-in-particular through her mouthpiece that connects to no-one-in-particular's inner ear.

No-one-in-particular says through the funnel that connects its outer mouth to the mother ship's largest ear, I know, but I'm not saying.

The mother ship retreats to her pillow space-cloud of soft debris. No-one-in-particular always knows but will not say, she thinks with a growing ire. Her internal temperature rises. She thrashes her fins. She spouts a fearsome fountain through her blowhole. She yells so loudly at no-one-in-particular that a shudder is felt through space/time. She feels her gallbladder filling.

When her gallbladder has become painfully distended, the mother ship releases the sac of bile into her goop. Her goop begins to froth. A bitter smell wafts from it. The grotesque child limps toward the goop. She dives in.

***

The eradication sphere is teeming with pests of every sort. It is blanketed in healthy weeds, flourished with fat roaches, scurried across with lush mice.

The pests from the eradication sphere have finished the construction of their vessels.

***

Now that she can swim daily in the mother ship's goop,
the grotesque child is completely grotesque again.

And now that the bile has returned to the mother ship's
goop, new children rise.

The new children call the grotesque child "tentacles-ben-tacles" and laugh at her distorted form.

While sleeping each night, the grotesque child dreams three vivid dreams.

Dream

She holds the stone cupped in her palms, it is smooth and yellow. She pulls her hands up to her mouth and breathes on the stone. The stone begins to squirm. It has soft, white fur, two black spots and a small black snout. It crawls all over her body, nesting in her recesses. You are like the animal, she tells the stone.

Dream

She is with a furry thing that wants to go into the fire-box. It is hard to keep the furry thing from going in to the firebox, but every time the furry thing approaches the hearth of the firebox, she pulls it back. The furry thing escapes her grasp and goes into the firebox. The healer is suddenly there. He says, Let the furry thing stay in the firebox, it knows what it needs to do. But she doesn't listen and pulls the furry thing out. When she pulls the furry thing out it is furless and spotless, like a newborn. She thinks she has made a mistake. She puts the furless thing back in the firebox. The furless thing burns. When the firebox cools down, the furless thing emerges. It is glossy black with honed edges.

Dream

The pests have joined together to make something glossy and dark. The glossy, dark thing they make is wise. They can separate themselves into weeds, roaches, and mice and still be part of the glossy black soul. When separated, they board the vessels in the eradication zone. The vessels are shaped like interstellar debris. The mother ship won't know, when she goes to her pillow space-cloud of soft debris that the vessels are there. They will latch onto the mother ship and be absorbed through her pores.

***

The grotesque child is never far from the animal. As the grotesque child walks, the animal curls around her neck like a scarf. The animal is white and furry with two dark spots. When the grotesque child puts her hands into the dark spots, her hands disappear. They connect to a deep muscle within the animal. The deep muscle contains muscle memory.

***

They came out through a small circle of light. They had been afraid in the sudden darkness. They had been so afraid that they trampled their own as they moved toward the small circle of light. When they finally emerged into the unknown world, they looked in vain for their missing ones. The beast has eaten them, they convinced themselves. The beast went one way to suckle its children. They went the other way, grieving for the trampled ones who never emerged, forgetting that they had been the ones who had trampled them.

They wandered the unknown world hating the beast.

***

The grotesque child and the animal are playing in the high hay. The high hay grows in the mother ship. It is harvested and put in the gristmill. The flour fuels the mother ship's engine.

The new children scamper about in the high hay.

They are not feeding from my milk tubes, the mother ship tells Brigit.

Brigit does not know how the new children can survive without the mother ship's milk. She goes into the high hay and secretly watches them. She sees them hunting in the high hay, stealthily catching mice and swallowing them whole.

Brigit wonders where the mice have come from.

The new children say, Here, tentacles-bentacles. When she limps toward them, they scamper off into the high hay.

The new children are mean to me, the grotesque child tells the mother ship.

I've noticed that this batch is cruel, worries the mother ship.

I'm glad I have the animal to play with.

Perhaps the new children are jealous, says the mother ship. None of them have an animal to play with.

The grotesque child plays with the animal. The animal likes to play hide and seek in the grotesque child's body. The grotesque child's body is filed with hiding places: nooks, crannies, recesses, and pockmarks.

Come out, come out wherever you are, sings the grotesque child to the animal.

When the animal is deep inside the grotesque child, it will release the moths. The moths keep the grotesque child free of hobgoblins so that the wind can continue to pass freely through her.

***

The grotesque child is playing with the animal in the high hay. The cruel children silently surround her. They hold the grotesque child down. The cruelest of the cruel children takes the animal.

Oh, what a sweet animal, says the cruelest cruel child. The other cruel children coo and caw. The cruelest cruel child hugs the animal. The animal whimpers. Please don't hug the animal too tight, begs the grotesque child. Too tight? asks the cruelest cruel child, You mean like this? And the cruelest cruel child hugs the animal so tight that it no longer whimpers. The other cruel children smirk and cackle.

The cruel child throws the limp body of the animal back to the grotesque child. Have fun playing with your animal, tentacles-bentacles, mocks the cruelest cruel child.

The Wise watches from the hay.

The grotesque child continues to wear her animal around her neck, but her animal slides off. She tries to play with her animal, but her animal does not play back.

Without the animal to feed her the daily moths, the grotesque child becomes internally ravaged by the wind.

Without the animal, the grotesque child no longer cares to swim in the mother ship's goop.

Without the animal, the grotesque child continuously emits a high-pitched wail.

Because she is no longer swimming in the goop, the grotesque child's feelers become ultra-sensitive again, but she does not notice the pain.

From a safe distance, the cruel children taunt her for her wind-ravaged form and her red-raw feelers. But the grotesque child's feelers extend from her. They seek the cold skin of a cruel child, wrap themselves around the cruel child's body, and squeeze the quench from the cruel child's icy blood.

The healer witnesses the grotesque child's actions. He tells the mother ship, Without the animal, the grotesque child is turning into the hideous child.

Every day the grotesque child's feelers find another cruel child to ensnarl. Then they savor the momentary quenching that the cruel child's icy blood provides.

***

The mother ship tries to convince the grotesque child to swim in her goop, but the grotesque child refuses.

The grotesque child continues to carry the animal. She has bound it with twine so that it will not fall from her. The animal rots around her neck and an aura of putrid smell surrounds the grotesque child and the decaying animal.

No one goes near the grotesque child.

The cruel children run from the grotesque child and her hideous form and nauseating smell and her deadly feelers.

***

I wish to abort the new children, the mother ship tells Brigit. There is something wrong with them she says. They killed the grotesque child's animal and her despair is deep and unending. Now that she won't swim in my goop, I don't know how to comfort her.

Where do you want to abort the new children? asks Brigit.

I would like to abort them onto one of the dead worlds. There is no hope for their survival there. Can you give me some medicine to help me?

Brigit agrees to give the mother ship the medicine to abort the new children because she has also noticed that the new children are particularly cruel. She has heard their vicious words and she has seen evidence of their torture in the abused forms of the others on the mother ship. She has noticed the new children's armor-like skin and their shallow eyes that hold light like frozen puddles.

Brigit collects a hair from each of the new children while they are sleeping. She weaves the hairs into a tight pill.

Here, take this, she says to the mother ship, handing her the tightly woven pill.

The mother ship travels to the dead worlds. They are stacked on top of each other. She squats on top of the tiered dead worlds. She swallows the tightly woven pill. She cries in pain as the new children are aborted onto the dead worlds.

The cruel children are gone, the mother ship tells the grotesque child. The grotesque child stares blankly and holds out her hands. Cupped in her hands are the bones of the animal.

I can't bear to see the grotesque child like this any longer, the mother ship cries to the healer. What can be done?

The healer has an idea. He takes some soft fabric and sews it into the likeness of the animal. He asks the grotesque child to hand him the bones of the animal. He takes the bones and grinds them with his mortar and pestle into a soft powder. He fills the fabric animal with the bone powder and sews it up. He hands the grotesque child the soft animal. The grotesque child gently hugs the animal. She says, I won't ever let anyone else hug you again.

The grotesque child is still internally ravaged by the wind, but her soft animal comforts her. She tentatively approaches the mother ship's goop. The mother ship says, Dive in.

***

On the eradication sphere, the pests had born a new species: a species of barbed weed and unexterminate-able roach and agile mouse. The new species was hardier and wiser than any of the old species. The old species in the eradication sphere gave up their singularity for the wholeness of the new species. The new species had an interlocking soul. The new species was called The Wise.

The Wise had secretly boarded the mother ship through her pores. After the Wise had boarded the mother ship, it had lost parts of its soul to the voracious appetites of the cruel children.

In order to be whole again, the Wise needed to find the pests from the old world.

***

The grotesque child follows the movement in the hay. She and the soft animal corner the movement against a wall. She cajoles the movement out. The movement is a spectacular crow holding something shiny in its beak.

Who are you? asks the grotesque child.
I am The Wise, says the spectacular crow.
What is that you're holding?
Here, look into it.

The grotesque child has never seen a mirror. The spectacular crow hands the mirror to the grotesque child. She looks into it.

The mirror is a window into the side-by-side world.

Grotesque child, what do you see?

I'm on a shore facing the beached whales. I go up to one of the still whales and breathe into it. It doesn't move so I crawl into its mouth.

What's inside?

There are star-like phosphorescent creatures dotting the whale's cavern. I see Ursa Major sleeping in the east. I see the animal approaching her.

Tell me more.

Before the sleeping bear fell asleep, the sleeping bear was awake. The awake bear ate berries and the awake bear gave birth to babies. She sheared her babies of all their hair and she made clothes for them. The awake bear sent her babies out to the New Place, and when her babies grew, they forgot that they came from the awake bear. When the awake bear came to the New Place to see her children, they shot her with a tranquilizer gun. The children brought the sleeping bear to the old place, far away from the New Place.

The New Place gradually inched up. Homes were built on top of homes to accommodate the children of the children. As the New Place got higher, the Industry that surrounded it got wider.

The sleeping bear sleeps in the old place and the animal lives in the New Place.

The sleeping bear is so big. The animal looks out from the middle floors of the New Place at the horizon and sees her. The sleeping bear starts with her head, which slopes down to her neck, which slopes up to her shoulders, which slopes further up to her belly, which slopes down to her legs, a little rise for her feet, and then the plains.

There is only one way to wake the sleeping bear.

The animal is one of the small ones. The animal is even smaller than the smallest small one. The animal is the very smallest one. The animal fits in a miniature dollhouse, a microcosm of a standard dollhouse. The animal sits on a miniature dollhouse chair and its feet don't even reach the floor.

The animal came from a small mother and a small father, but they were much bigger than it. The animal was born smaller than a small baby. The animal's mother did not even know she was pregnant, did not even know she had given birth until the father said, "What is that thing dangling from you?" And the mother pulled the thread-like cord that hung from between her legs and saw the animal on the end suspended like a spider.

The sleeping bear is big to everyone, even the giants that live next door. The giant neighbor says, "I won't go near the sleeping bear." And the animal says, "I'm going to wake the sleeping bear," and the giant neighbor says, "What?" And places the animal in his ear canal.

The giant neighbor's ear canal has these thick hairs like tree trunks and the animal often gets lost in the stands. The animal tells the giant neighbor again, "I am going to wake the sleeping bear." Then the animal tries to find its way out of the ear canal. After many disoriented minutes, the animal shouts and sees the tip of a big finger parting the stands. The animal jumps on the finger and the giant neighbor removes the animal from his ear canal. This is how they converse.

How does the animal know how to wake the sleep-ing bear? The animal's knowledge of how to wake the sleeping bear is innate in it, like its very smallness. If it had been born normal-sized, it would not know how to wake the sleeping bear.

The animal spends a lot of its time planning, looking out over the Industry. There is tight security around the borders. There are large, central buildings that are shrouded in the thick smoke of burning grease. The animal's parents want to know why it spends so many hours by the window when there is nothing to see but variegated smog.

Up above the sleeping bear is the old sky. It seeps light onto the bear in the day and it hangs the old moon over the bear at night. The old night sky also has these tiny spots of brightness that the animal would like to nestle into. In the New Place, the night sky is constantly dusked by the lights from the Industry that surrounds it on all sides. In the New Place, the day sky is dusked by the smoke that perpetually exhales from the Industry.

To get to the sleeping bear the animal must go through
the Industry.

The animal tells its mother that it wants to go for a walk. The mother gently tightens the animal's miniature gas mask. She brushes back the sprigs of its hair that grow like blighted crops from the animal's scalp. She rubs cream into the animal's skin that is in a constant state of slough; the animal's body wants to renew itself, but the raw nutrients that assist this process have long been leached from the New Place. The animal keeps shedding its skin with no fresh skin to replace it.

The animal secretly carries a small sack of provisions: murky water and a bag of kibble that is made from the indeterminate substance that is manufactured in the Industry.

No one wants to go into the Industry, but the workers will sometimes go to great lengths to escape. The animal is so small that it is easy for it to pass through security, undetected. The Industry smells of suffering. No one can say what happens there. The smell is a mixture of burnt flesh and ammonia and sulfur and a strong rotting smell that emanates from the central buildings. These central buildings shift and heave and moan.

It takes days for the animal to traverse the Industry. The animal does not sleep or eat. The animal notices a similar starved and fatigued quality about the workers. They drift through the Industry like litter in the breeze.

The animal comes to the outside perimeter of the Industry. There is a wide expanse of cropland growing the same blighted crops as lusterless as the fur on the animal's body. The soil is ashen, and when the animal picks it up, its paws tingle. The soil is clearly bereft of all fertility, and it has the same strong smell of rotting that comes from the central buildings in the Industry. The crops grow rot-mottled grains from their spindly stalks. The animal thinks of its kibble.

The animal trudges through the fields lined with rows and rows of this one bleak plant.

The animal comes to the edge of the crops. A giant hedgerow obscures the view beyond. It is tightly tangled in brambles that endeavor to grow berries. But they, too, are marred by rot and dusted in ashy soil.

The brambles are so tightly snarled that it is difficult for the animal to find passage. The thorns are profuse and barbed. The animal has no tool with it. No weapon. Everything the animal has to do must be done with its bare hands. The animal begins the painful task of rooting through. The thorns seek its blood. The animal feels the hedgerow tightening around it, crushing its small bones, putting its barbs through the animal like teeth. The animal thinks of the sleeping bear. The animal imagines crawling into her ear canal and whispering to her the story of the Industry and the New Place. The animal then goes deeper into the sleeping bear's ear, right against her eardrum. The animal pounds and yells, "It is not a dream! You must wake up! It is not a dream."

The grotesque child wakes up in the high hay next to
The Wise.

Wise, she asks, did the sleeping bear ever wake?

***

Healer, what is your vision?

The mother ship was asleep beneath the water while Ursa was plumping up a cloud to rest her head on. I was on the land and I held a bowl of fluttering moths in my stomach. In my pocket, I kept a snail shell. The night was soon to be. It bothered me how high it went, the night sky. Once it had been a roof.

I thought about the voices I heard. The voices without mouths. I asked no-one-in-particular, Why can't I understand them?

I pitched my tent. It was an old tent, threadbare, inviting in the wind and stars. I slept a sleep that could hear the mother ship: she thrashed all night beneath the water. I slept a sleep that could see Ursa: she tossed and turned on her pillow. I took off my ear and put the snail shell in its place. The voices came back and I understood them; they told me to go to the shore.

Ursa had fallen into the water, which was speckled in phosphorescent dots. I found the mother ship beached in the sand. I birthed the bowl of moths through my mouth. I held the bowl to the mother ship's lips and said, Drink. But the mother ship was unresponsive. I opened her mouth and poured the moths down her throat. The mother ship stirred. Then she began to rise.

Ursa washed to shore. I gathered her phosphorescence in my palm. I held the bowl with moths in my other hand. I tipped the bowl toward the phosphorescence and said, Drink. Moments later a great bear stood before me.

How did you become a healer?

I was born both doctor and healer. As a young child, the doctor and healer were in unison, the line between them blurred. In school, we learned how bad healers were. They used herbs and superstition instead of chemicals and science, our teacher said. Healers are irrational beings our teacher told us. They used intuition instead of logic, emotions instead of reason. Whenever I chanted in class, my teacher would make me eat a scalding pepper. Whenever I healed a classmate with a poultice, my teacher said it was a fluke. Gradually I absorbed the healer deep inside me and pushed the doctor to my surface. Everyone loved the doctor. The doctor went on to get diplomas and certificates. The doctor ended up at a research facility where the mechanics of pain were studied.

The other doctors in the research facility said, This is the most important work being done today. We might learn how to eradicate pain completely. Imagine a pain free existence for everyone!

In the meantime, the pain we inflicted on our subjects was extreme and unconscionable. I could feel the scream of our subjects boring beneath my doctor-self and penetrating into the healer.

At night, the healer would come out. It would absorb the doctor self into its center. The nightmares were unbearable.

When we captured the child and brought her to the research facility, the person of unquestionable authority said that we were going to remove the sheaths from the child's feelers. We had never seen feelers on a child, and he thought we could learn how the substance might protect our own nerves. And the person of unquestionable authority wanted to know what amount of pain the child could endure before dying.

As we stood over the convulsing child, I felt the child's feelers extend invisible threads that bored into my doctor-self, grasped hold of the healer and began to pull the healer out.

The doctor did not let the healer out without a fight. The doctor poked one of my eyes through my eye socket and deep into my head. And the doctor screeched into one of my ears until the drum burst.

I emerged as the partially blinded and deaf healer.

***

The grotesque child looks out the porthole of the mother ship. She sees the space debris circling an orbit. She sees the dead worlds in the distance: their deep scars brimmed with shadows. The grotesque child looks next to her in bed at the soft animal. The grotesque child takes the soft animal and lays it next to her head on the pillow.

The soft animal sings her a lullaby. The grotesque child feels the mother ship dissolve around her.

There is a beast that lives by the dry wash. The beast has soft, curly hair, a long tongue, small branches that grow from its head like antlers, and snail shell ears. The dry wash has been dry for as long as anyone can remember and the villagers that live by it are thirsty. I tell the villagers that if someone were able to get one of the snail shell ears from the beast and bring it back to the village, all the villagers would be able to imagine the dry wash flowing with water.

The dry wash is lined with picnic tables and that is where the villagers sit to have their picnics. They watch the dry wash and try to imagine it flowing with water. But no matter how good their imaginations, they can't see the dry wash flowing with water.

I have the best imagination of anyone, but even I can't look at the dry wash and see it flowing with water.

I am the only one that can imagine the beast, though. No one else has ever imagined the beast, but the way I describe it, no one doubts me. The villagers ask me, "Can you go to the beast and find out how we might get one of its snail shell ears?"

I leave the picnic tables and go to a small clearing in the forest. It is the place where my imagination works best. I sit in the position that makes my imagination work best. I hum a discordant tune. When the others hear the discordant tune coming from the forest, they will know that I am going deep within my imagination and soon I will be able to tell them how to gain one of the snail shell ears.

The beast is sitting with its back against the tree. The beast has a fishing pole and I watch as it pulls fish after fish from the dry wash. "How are you able to catch fish in the dry wash?" I ask the beast. The beast turns its head, and I can more clearly see one of the beast's snail shell ears, and I see that the ear is lined with mother of pearl. I ask the beast, "May I hold your ear?" The beast puts down its fishing pole and gently takes off its ear and hands it to me. I look at the iridescent interior and feel my sight drain into it. When I take my eyes away from the snail shell ear, I see a wide river coursing where the dry wash had been.

The beast asks for its ear back, but I say, "I just want to hold it for a little bit longer." and I put it in my pocket. Then I go and find a stick and fashion it into a fishing pole. I sit with the beast on the banks of the wide river.

I notice a sensation on my shoulder. Someone is tapping me and I look up and see one of the villagers and he says, "Grotesque child, you have been imagining for days. Can you tell us how to get one of the snail shell ears from the beast?"

"No," I say, "I need more time to imagine and I need to not be disturbed." So the others build a shelter around

119

me so that I can imagine without being disturbed. They build the shelter without doors or windows so that no one can enter. They drill a small hole into the top to allow in a thin shaft of light. They do not want me to be in utter darkness when I am roused from my imagining.

The beast and I sit on the banks of the wide river and catch so many fish and we catch the fish without harming them. The beast and I release the fish and the fish grow legs and run off into the forest.

"I want to see where those fish are going," I tell the beast. The beast says, "I wouldn't do that." And I say, "But you're a beast and you're not afraid of anything." And the beast says, "Ha!" Which unsettles me because I imagine that the beast is not afraid of anything.

"Why are we catching these fish?" I ask the beast, and the beast says, "We are catching them to eat." And I say, "No, we are releasing them and they are running off into the forest." And the beast says, "Why don' t you smell your own breath." And I cup my hand over my mouth and nose and breathe out and my breath stinks of fish.

I look at the beast and see its curly hair squirming around, and for the first time I notice the beast's hair is actually a tangle of earthworms.

"I don't believe anything you say!" I yell at the beast, and I throw my fishing pole at the beast and I can see, vividly, the blood that coats the sharp hook. "I'm going to find those fish that have run off into the forest!"

I run and run and I catch glimpses of the fish and they are beginning to look like my own people. I see them sitting at the picnic tables, staring into the dry wash. "I have the answer!" I call out to them, but they do not look my way.

I go back into the forest and find the clearing. I sit in the position where my imagination works best, and I begin to hum the discordant tune.

I look around and see that I am in an unfamiliar space. It has one hole bored into the top that lets in enough light for me to make out my surroundings. I can see that there are no doors or windows. I yell out, "I have the answer, I know how to get the snail shell ear. The beast is so kind; I just asked the beast if I could hold its ear and it gave it to me."

I hope that the villagers will hear the good news and release me.

The shelter shudders again and again and I am happy because the villagers have heard me and have come to save me. But when the shelter finally collapses, only the beast stands there.

*I look at the beast's hair and see that it is soft and curly.
I pet the beast and the beast purrs. I reach into my pocket
and hand the beast its snail shell ear. The beast attaches its
ear and says, "Follow me."*

*The beast takes me to the banks of the dry wash. There
is no water in it, only sand, rippled in tiny waves by the
wind. "I should go back to my people," I tell the beast.*

*"I wouldn't do that," says the beast. And I look around
more closely and I see the bones of my people scattered on
the banks of the dry wash, some of them with rusted hooks
lodged in their jaws.*

The grotesque child wakes up gasping with sobs. As her breath returns, slowly the mother ship materializes around her. On the pillow next to her head, she sees the soft animal. The grotesque child picks it up and carefully examines it. She notices for the first time that the soft animal's ears are snail shells.

The grotesque child whispers into the soft animals snail shell ear, Who is the beast?

***

No-one-in-particular is no-where-in-particular. No-one-in-particular wishes it could be someone and somewhere. It is tiring to be in a constant state of no/all being. No-one-in-particular decides to dig a hole for itself in the sky: A place where it can be. Once no-one-in-particular begins digging a hole for itself, it finds that the hole in never big enough to contain it. So the hole gets deeper and wider.

Things begin to fall into the hole.

***

The grotesque child tells the mother ship, I am concerned about no-one-in-particular.

The mother ship says, I am too. It keeps digging and digging and more and more keeps falling into it.

The grotesque child looks out the porthole. In the distance she can see star after star falling into no-one-in-particular's hole.

***

No one has seen the healer for days.

The grotesque child goes to the healer's vent and finds him crouched there. The healer does not look well. The grotesque child listens to the healer's chest. She hears a clanging, then a thrum thrum, then a sputtering.

Where is it coming from? asks the healer weakly.

I think it is coming from deep inside you, says the grotesque child.

Who will heal the healer? asks the healer.

The grotesque child thinks, The midwife will heal the healer.

The grotesque child summons Brigit to the healer's vent. Brigit looks at the healer's tongue. She examines the whites of his eyes. She bites him gently with her teeth and tastes his blood. She smells the mucous that runs from his nose. She listens to the myriad sounds churning and popping and gushing within him. She kneads her hands deep into his viscera.

What is the prognosis? Asks the grotesque child.

An integral part of the healer is in danger, says Brigit.

Inside the healer, the long buried doctor has begun to metastasize.

How will you heal the healer? The grotesque child asks Brigit.

I can't heal the healer, says Brigit, Something the healer repressed a long time ago is eating its way out.

***

Brigit notices that the grotesque child is sprouting tiny bulbs in rows down her chest. It is time for me to work inside the grotesque child, thinks Brigit.

While the grotesque child sleeps, Brigit works inside her. Brigit massages her fallopian tubes. Brigit lines her uterus with plush fabric and deposits three golden eggs within her ovaries.

The grotesque child wakes up. She feels a weight in her center. She reaches between her legs and pulls out a bright red scarf. She ties the scarf around her waist. The grotesque child feels steadier with the weight in her center and the scarf around her waist.

The grotesque child goes to the healer who is now delirious. The healer says over and over again, The cruel children have built a machine. The grotesque child unties the scarf from her waist and wipes the perspiration from the healer's brow. He looks at her with translucent eyes and says, The dead worlds are alive.

***

The cruel children landed on the dead worlds and for days did not know what to do. It was clear that if they didn't do something, they would all die.

Georgie was the smartest and the cruelest of the cruel children and he pulled together a particularly cruel bunch of children and he called them his disciples. He told his disciples, We will kill the other cruel children and eat them. We will mix their bones and gristle with dead soil and the soil will be revived.

Georgie and his disciples told the other children that hey were being sacrificed to bring the dead worlds back to life. Georgie slit each of their throats and let their blood flow through the ashen soil like a river.

Georgie and his disciples grew fat off the children's tender meat. The soil in the dead worlds turned deep and rich. The seeds that had lain dormant in the dead soil began to sprout. Within months, the dead worlds were forested.

***

A pod flies around the mother ship. The mother ship says to the grotesque child, Who is in the pod?

Now that the grotesque child wears the red scarf, she can see beyond the walls.

It is one of your children who has come back, the grotesque child tells the mother ship.

The mother ship pulls the pod into the receiving chamber. The doors of the pod open and there stands one of the new children who is now old. The mother ship asks, Why have you come back?

The old child says, Can I rest first? I am terribly old and tired.

And it is true, the old child is frail and knotted and cataracted.

The grotesque child takes the old child to the resting chamber and tucks her in bed. Thank you grotesque child, says the old child. And then the old child dies.

More pods come and more old children step out and more old children die in the resting chamber.

We need the healer, says the mother ship to the grotesque child.

The grotesque child has not told the mother ship about the healer's illness. The healer is barely breathing. The healer is floating in his own sweat. The healer is murmuring about the cruel children. You must stop them, he tells the grotesque child.

The mother ship has been watching the stars tumble into no-one-in-particular's hole. We don't have much time until no-one-in-particular's hole is wide enough for us to fall into

We need the healer, says the mother ship. Why won't he answer me?

The healer is near death. The grotesque child finally tells the mother ship about his illness. The prognosis is not good, she tells the mother ship. The mother ship is beside her self with worry.

The grotesque child goes into the chamber that is the mother ship's mind. The chamber is dark and the air is heavy. The tiny phosphorescent creatures that blink from ceiling of the mother ship's mind chamber have fallen to the floor and are dimming.

The grotesque child tries to unshutter one of the portholes to let some star light into the mother ship's mind chamber, but the shutters are clasped shut and no prying will open them.

We must stop the cruel children, the healer says.

How? Asks the grotesque child.

I must visit the side-by-side world, says the healer, and then he finishes his last breath.

The mother ship feels a dead weight in the healer's vent. Her mind chamber darkens.

The mother ship is inconsolable. The grotesque child brings a torch into the mother ship's mind chamber, but the heavy air extinguishes the torch as soon as she enters. The mother ship's mind is pitch dark. The grotesque child quickly leaves. She is afraid she could become permanently lost in the mother ship's dark mind.

The grotesque child goes to the mother ships' heart chamber. There she encounters a sluggish machine. The mother ship's heart is so old, the grotesque child thinks. And now with the healer dead and the growing hole of no-one-in-particular, how will we survive?

The grotesque child takes the scarf from around her waist. It is slightly stiff with the perspiration of the healer. She ties the scarf around one of the tubes leading to the mother ship's heart. The heart begins to beat faster as the perspiration from the healer is absorbed through the tube and into the mother ship's blood.

The grotesque child goes back to the mother ship's mind chamber. She is able to open the shutters on the porthole. Outside the porthole is a moon. Its light fills the mind chamber with a calm blue luminosity.

That moon looks familiar, thinks the grotesque child.

***

The grotesque child tells the mother ship, Brigit has put something inside me. There is a heaviness in my center.

The mother ship says to Brigit, Why did you put something inside the grotesque child? She is not old enough!

Brigit says, I put three golden eggs inside the grotesque child. She will soon need to find her mate.

***

On the dead worlds that are now alive, Georgie and his disciples have been busy making machines of growing complexity. The dead worlds that are now alive are filled with every ore imaginable. And with the thick forests and dark seams of coal and deep pockets of oil, there is no stopping their progress.

Georgie tells his disciples, We are going to build a ship bigger than the mother ship. Our ship will spawn cruel children. We are going to take our ship into the sky and kill the mother ship.

***

The grotesque child places the red scarf on her forehead. She places the soft animal next to her. She whispers into the soft animals snail shell ear, Where is the beast? The mother ship begins to dissolve around her.

***

When you woke up, you found me nearly dead in the brambles. You nursed me back to health. You fed me food from the old world and I grew big and strong. My fur grew back, soft and shiny. My snout glistened and my eyes shone bright. We sat together in the old world and watched a dark cloud grow out from the new world.

You remembered what your children had done to you and you were angry with them. You disowned your children. You said that disowning them would make it easier for you to do what you had to do. When I asked you what you had to do, you said you had to destroy your children who had made the industry.

On the night of the new moon, when the old world was its darkest, you summoned your rage. Your fur began to squirm. Your eyes turned lightless and could penetrate the blackness. Antlers grew from your head like trees. Your ears could hear beyond the old world and into the new.

You then taught me how to summon my rage. We set out for the new world.

The new world was bright in the darkness. The light disoriented you. You had never seen the small suns that illuminated the night.

I knew about the new world. I called the suns lamps and we followed the paths I called streets.

It would be easy to dismantle this rootless place, you knew. You summoned your rage again and began to stomp up and down. The new world trembled and shook. Your disowned children emerged from their houses. They cried in dismay as the new world tumbled down in the quakes.

You then sucked in all the wind of the new world into your lungs. Your chest inflated out, out, out, and you began to rise. Then you exhaled the wind into a ferocious swirl that further devastated the new world, flattening the crumbled buildings to the ground.

Then you went up into the clouds, drinking all their moisture. For days you hovered in the sky, spewing out the moisture through your fangs.

The new world was brought down by your quakes and leveled by your wind and sunk by your flood. Some of your children managed to survive and they floated below us and when they saw you in the sky, they said, mother bear, please forgive us.

You forgave your surviving children. We came down from the sky and the children climbed onto our backs and we brought them back to the old world.

Is the old world still there? the grotesque child asks the soft animal.

The old world will always be.

***

The grotesque child looks out the porthole. No-one-in-particular is still there. She watches as the familiar moon teeters on the edge of no-one-in-particular's hole.

The grotesque child motions to no-one-in-particular through the porthole. She catches no-one-in-particular's attention right before the moon falls in.

The grotesque child gets on a pod and goes to no-one-in-particular. No-one-in-particular's dust spiral eyes have calmed to pale blue pools. The grotesque child looks into no-one-in-particular's calm pools and sees her reflection. She asks no-one-in-particular, Is this what I look like?

This is what you look like to me, says no-one-in-particular.

No-one-in-particular, says the grotesque child, I'm afraid that if you keep digging your hole, everything is going to fall into it.

The hole is getting quite crowded, says no-one-in-particular, but where will I be if not in this hole?

You could try fitting into one of my nooks or crannies, says the grotesque child. I will put my red scarf back inside for you to use as a blanket.

No-one-in-particular stops digging and goes into one of the grotesque child's nooks. No-one-in-particular is exhausted after all its digging. No-one-in-particular curls up under the red scarf and falls asleep.

Things stop falling into the hole.

***

Georgie and his disciples name their ship the Grande Dame. The Grande Dame is as big as the dead worlds that are now alive. Georgie's disciples journeyed to the dead worlds that are now alive and built each part of the Grande Dame, gradually connecting all the parts.

Georgie calls his disciples together in the hull of the Grande Dame. We have everything we need on the Grande Dame, and we have stripped the dead worlds that are now alive so that now they are dead again.

Georgie and his disciples launch the Grande Dame into space. Watch this, says Georgie and he pushes a button. Through the observation window Georgie and his disciples watch as the dead worlds that were once alive and then died again are blown to bits.

***

On the mother ship, a shock is felt. What was that? asks the mother ship.

***

With Georgie at the helm, the Grande Dame races toward the mother ship.

***

The old children continue to flock to the mother ship to die inside her.

Oh how I wish the healer was still alive, she tells no-one-in-particular.

***

The healer is now in the side-by-side world. From the side-by-side world he can see the world next to him. He can see a tremendous ship coming toward the mother ship at an alarming rate.

In the side-by-side world, the healer is joined by the old children who had come back to the mother ship to die inside her. He is joined by the cruel children that Georgie murdered. He is joined by the animal.

The sacrificed cruel children in the side-by-side world say, Now we see Georgie for who he really is, and they denounce their cruelty.

The old children are lithe and agile in the side-by-side world.

The animal is wild and beastly in the side-by-side world.

The healer has two far seeing eyes and two wide hearing ears.

Everyone in the side-by-side world can see the other worlds next to the side-by-side world.

The healer scans the side-by-side world with his far-seeing sight. To the east, he sees a large bear and her cubs. We must go east, he tells the animal/beast, the old children who are now agile and lithe, and the sacrificed cruel children who are no longer cruel.

***

The remnants of the industry slowly became overcome with weeds. From the weeds emerged the mice. From the rubble emerged the roaches.

In the old world, Ursa was with her children. At night they saw the ceiling of stars. In the day they drank water from the streams and they ate berries that grew fat from the brambles. They knew no predator.

It went on like this until one of the children grew curious about what was beyond the brambles. The curious child decided she would go on an adventure to the other side of the brambles and then come back and tell her story to the other children, and to Ursa, who would be very proud.

The curious child walked to the edge of the old world and came to the brambles. The brambles said to the curious child, Halt! Who goes there?

It is me; I'm just a curious child.

What are you curious about? asked the brambles.

I am curious about what is on the other side of you, said the curious child.

Why are you curious? asked the brambles.

I now know every inch of the old world and I wonder what is on the other side of you. Maybe there is something magnificent there that I can see. Then I can come back and tell new stories to Ursa and the other children.

Are you sure you want new stories? asked the brambles.

Yes, said the curious child.

Very well then, said the brambles, and the brambles opened a small hole that the curious child could pass through.

The curious child walked into the ruins of the new worlds. The ruins were covered in bright and tenacious weeds. In a few moments, she was surrounded by large mice and even larger roaches.

What are you doing here? asked the pests.

I am looking for a new story to tell Ursa and the children in the old world.

Come with us, said the pests, we have a story for you.

The curious child followed the pests to their lair. Their lair was dark and dank and musky. The pests built a fire and she could see that the walls of the lair were covered with paintings. In the depths of the cave, she could now see a painting of a spectacular crow.

Who is that? she whispered.

That is The Wise, said the pests. We want to find The Wise and be included in the Wise's interlocking soul. These paintings are a prophecy that will lead us to The Wise.

The paintings showed two great ships battling in space.

This is what we are waiting for, said the pests.

The pests told the curious child the story of the two great ships. When the pests got to the end, the curious child asked, What happened next?

We don't know, said the pests.

After the story of the two great ships, the curious child fell asleep in the pests' lair. Because she was so tired, she slept for days.

***

After traveling east for days, the healer and his party encounter some children playing nearby.

The beast sees the children and says to the healer, Those are my siblings.

Ursa's children see a group approaching them. They see many curious figures in the group, and among them, someone they recognize.

They run toward the healer and his party. They surround the beast.

***

After we rescued my surviving children and carried them on our backs to the old world, I left you to fend for yourself. I had taught you how to summon your rage and become the beast. I was sure it would protect you. You needed to be separated from me. You had to find the grotesque child. It was not my choice. It was what no-one-in-particular had ordained.

I left you near a boulder that was my size and shape.

***

The beast introduces Ursa's children to the healer.

We must talk to Ursa, he tells Ursa's children.

Come with us, say the children. Each of them fight to hold the beast's paws as they walk toward Ursa.

Ursa sees a group coming toward her. She sees her own children. She sees the healer who gave her a land-body. She sees many children that she does not recognize. Her own children are vying for the attention of a figure in their midst. She looks closer to see that the figure is the one who woke her.

The beast sees Ursa. Ursa is the size and shape of the boulder the beast grew up under. The beast sees Ursa. The beast thinks, Ursa is my real mother.

The beast and Ursa embrace. Your rage has transformed you, says Ursa to the beast.

After you left, says the beast, I was the animal. I kept the beast in my dark recesses. When the bright light entered me, it began to illuminate the beast. The grotesque child was with me. She fed me the seeds of the night-food. The night-food sprouted and grew inside me. The night-food grew shade over the beast.

The grotesque child and I were inseparable. I kept her wind channels clean with a daily dose of moths and she kept my recesses shaded by tending to my night seeds.

After the grotesque child endured unspeakable torture at the hands of our captors, the healer rescued us. Eventually, we were taken by the mother ship into her hull.

We lived for years in the mother ship. I would either curl around the grotesque child's neck, or hide in one of her nooks.

From the mother ship's goop came her children. There was a batch born that was cruel. They taunted the grotesque child. They envied her because she had me. One day, the cruelest of the cruel children crushed me in an embrace.

As I was being crushed, I felt the night-food seeds die. I felt the brightness inside me fully illuminate the beast in my recesses.

When I emerged in the side-by-side world, I was the beast.

The beast says to its real mother, I need to return to the animal. Ursa says, You must eat the soft animal in order to return to the animal.

***

It is good to see you again, says the healer to Ursa.

And you, too, says Ursa, The last time I saw you, I had fallen into the ocean and you gave me my animal body. Since then, I've lived in the old world.

I sense that something troubles you, says the healer.

One of my children has been missing for days. I fear she has gone to the new world. The brambles will not let me pass into the new world, and I won't send any of my children there.

I'll go to the new world and find the lost child, says the healer.

The healer approaches the brambles.

Halt! Who goes there? asks the brambles.

It is the healer.

Why do you wish to pass?

I am looking for a curious child who has become lost. Have you seen her?

I let a curious child pass through here many days ago, says the brambles.

Why did you let her pass? asks the healer.

She was looking for a new story to tell Ursa and the other children.

May I pass to find her and bring her back? We need to hear her story.

Only if you can heal me, says the brambles.

Deep within the brambles is a dead spot. In the dead spot, the berries are shriveled, the leaves brown, and the thorns brittle.

I must continue to protect the passage from the old world into the new world and vise-versa. This dead spot is growing, says the brambles. Soon, anyone will be able to pass whether or not they are ready.

The healer takes out his vial of phosphorescence. He says to the brambles, Drink. He pours the phosphorescence into the roots of the dead spot.

The dead spot begins to revitalize. The berries plump up, the leaves turn bright green, the thorns strengthen to razor-barbs.

You may pass through, says the brambles.

The healer arrives in the new world. He sees the remnants of the industry. He sees the brilliantly colored weeds growing thick over the remnants.

Soon, the healer is surrounded by large mice and even larger roaches.

I am looking for a curious child, he tells them.

Why do you search for her? they ask.

Her mother, Ursa, Is worried about her. And she also has come here for a new story. We need to hear her story.

Come with us, say the pests.

The curious child is fast asleep in the lair. The healer gently nudges her.

Where am I? she asks as she wakes.

You are in the pests' lair, says the healer.

Now I remember. They have told me a new story without ending.

Come back with me to the old world so you can tell us your story, says the healer.

Everyone is sitting around the curious child and they are rapt with attention. Even the brambles in the distance are listening closely.

There were two great sky-ships, begins the curious child. One sky-ship had flippers and a blowhole. This sky-ship had birthed many, many, children and the many births had taken their toll on the sky-ship. This sky-ship began to deteriorate. This sky-ship worried about who would birth the new children after she was gone.

On this sky-ship lived a peculiar child. This was the only child that the sky-ship had not born. This peculiar child and the sky-ship found each other in one of the many worlds the sky-ship visited. The sky-ship was looking for this child.

This child could barely live on the world where the sky-ship found her. The world was too harsh and this peculiar child was too sensitive. The peculiar child could live on the mother ship, but she was crooked and had deep nooks and crannies. She had cysts and pockmarks. She had hair that grew from her scalp in wispy tufts.

The other sky-ship was brand new. It was the size of many worlds. It fiercely glistened. It had an impenetrable shell. This sky-ship was capable of birthing many, many fierce and hardened children.

This sky-ship was captained by the cruelest of the cruel. He had been born from the other sky-ship. The other sky-ship was afraid of his cruelty and aborted him unto the dead worlds that had once been alive.

The dead worlds that had once been alive had once been profoundly beautiful. There were deep forests and high mountains and undulating deserts and soft grasslands and wide clear rivers. At first, the people of these worlds were content. But gradually they began to notice things that displeased them. One person decided the weeds needed to go. Another was tired of the mice. Another still was rallying against the roaches. The people said, Wouldn't these worlds be perfect without these pests? The people of these worlds gathered up all the pests and sent them to the eradication zone. Little did they know that the beauty of their worlds depended on these pests. First the plants began to die. Then the animals. The people tried to save their worlds, but they succumbed as well.

The dead worlds that had once been alive suited the cruel children. They learned, through great atrocities, to survive. They brought the dead worlds back to life. Then they took all the new life from the worlds and used it to make their sky-ship.

The cruelest of the cruel children and the cruel children who revered him, manned the sky-ship. Their task was to destroy the other sky-ship, their mother.

What happened next, everyone wants to know.

Next has yet to happen, says the curious child.

The healer tells Ursa and her children, I have come from the first sky-ship. As we speak, the new sky-ship approaches her. Ursa, I need the help of you and your children.

Of course, says Ursa.

I'll help too, says the brambles. And from beyond the brambles the pests say, We will also help.

***

The Grande Dame births her first litter. Georgie looks through the litter methodically. The children are perfectly fierce and perfectly armored. But under the writhing litter, Georgie finds a soft child. This child will not do, Georgie tells the Grande Dame, and he plucks the soft child from the Grande Dame's milk tube.

Please spare the soft child, says the Grande Dame.

Are you showing compassion? asks Georgie. We did not program you to feel compassion.

Georgie is worried about the Grande Dame.

One of Georgie's disciples is a nice child posing as a cruel child.

Georgie calls his disciples to the interrogation chamber. Someone has programmed compassion into the Grande Dame. I will methodically torture each of you until I find out who has done it.

Georgie tortures the cruel children. He burns them with boiling oil. He drills into their teeth. He plays loud music and keeps them from sleep. The cruel children tell him nothing because they know nothing.

Georgie calls Jeffery into the torture chamber. Jeffery hates that the others were tortured, but he knows it must be this way.

Georgie says to Jeffery, You are one of the most popular children. The other children like to talk to you, I've noticed. I believe you know something about who programmed compassion into the Grande Dame.

No, Sir, says Jeffery, I know nothing.

I'm giving you four days to find out. If I don't know by then, I'll kill you, then all the cruel children, and then I will eat the soft child.

***

The healer devises a plan to get Ursa, her children, the pests, and the brambles back to the world where the mother ship is.

The healer asks the animal/beast to hand him his healer's bag. The bag holds four implements: a knife, a spoon, a bowl, and a spindle of thread. The healer asks the brambles to hold Ursa down and to intoxicate her with its heady flower scent. Ursa is soon deep in sleep. The healer cuts open Ursa's soft belly with the knife. He spoons out the moths that flutter within Ursa. He spoons the moths into his bowl. When he has removed all of the moths from Ursa, Ursa begins to come apart in large clumps that then break down into smaller clumps that then break down into specks of phosphorescence.

The healer then ties Ursa's children to the specks of phosphorescence. He ties the brambles and the pests to the specks. He ties himself and the beast to the specks. He ties the old children who are now agile and lithe to the specks, and he ties the sacrificed cruel children who are no longer cruel to the specks.

After everyone has been tied to the phosphorescent specks of Ursa, the healer instructs the moths to fly them all to the sky where the mother ship floats.

The moths carry the specks of phosphorescence to the sky where the mother ship lives. They place the specks very carefully in the sky. They leave Ursa's children with her in the sky. Then they untie the other passengers and carry them toward the mother ship.

The grotesque child looks out the porthole. She sees specks of phosphorescence taking form in the sky. The specks form the shape of a bear.

Mother ship, do you see what is taking form in the sky? she asks the mother ship.

Yes, says the mother ship. It is my old friend Ursa.

The mother ship and the grotesque child then see that there are moths in the sky carrying passengers toward the mother ship's receiving chamber.

The receiving chamber's door open. The grotesque child is waiting there. The moths land, and from them disembark the healer, the beast, the pests, the brambles, the old children who are now agile and lithe, and the sacrificed cruel children who are no longer cruel.

The grotesque child sees the beast and trembles. Her soft animal stirs. Why are you stirring? she whispers to the soft animal.

The soft animal suddenly leaps from the grotesque child's shoulders. The soft animal approaches the beast timidly. The beast picks up the soft animal and engulfs it.

The grotesque child screams.

The beast softens before everyone's eyes. The antlers recede. The squirming earthworms turn to lush fur.

The grotesque child sees that the beast has transformed into the animal that Georgie killed.

The animal goes back to the grotesque child and crawls into one of her nooks.

The animal finds no-one-in-particular sleeping in the grotesque child's nook. No-one-in-particular wakes and sees the animal. The animal asks, is there enough room for me in this nook? Climb in and we'll see, says no-one-in-particular.

No-one-in-particular and the animal talk to each other in the nook. The animal learns about no-one-in-particular's hole digging. No-one-in-particular hears about the threat to the mother ship. I need to board the enemy ship that threatens the mother ship, but I don't know how, says the animal. Talk to Brigit, says no-one-in-particular. The animal exits the grotesque child's nook in search of Brigit.

The animal finds Brigit and tells her that it needs to board the enemy ship that threatens the mother ship. Brigit loosens her mind and lets it drift over to the Grande Dame. Her loosened mind inhales the scent of the Grande Dame and tastes the sweat of the Grande Dame and feels every mountain and valley of the Grande Dame and listens, intently to the nuances of the Grande Dame's every breath.

Brigit's loose mind floats back to her and tightens in her head.

I've found a breach, she tells the animal.

There is a chink in the soft child's head through which the animals' mind can enter.

The animal attenuates its mind into an invisible thread. The thread drifts across space and enters the chink in the soft child's mind.

***

Georgie has taken the soft child into his quarters. He finds it comforting to tell the soft child about his troubles.

Someone has programmed compassion into the Grande Dame's mind chamber. My mission will not succeed if the Grande Dame feels even an iota of compassion, he tells the soft child.

The soft child looks at Georgie with soft eyes.

I don't like it when you do that, he says, and he takes a sharp object and pokes it into one of the soft child's soft eyes.

Georgie takes the soft child that is whimpering and bleeding out of its eye to Jeffery.

Pitiful isn't it, Georgie says to Jeffery.

I think the soft child might know something about where the Grande Dame's compassion came from, says Jeffery.

The soft child can't talk, says Georgie.

Nevertheless, says Jeffery, I would like to try to communicate with it.

Very well, says Georgie.

Who are you? asks Jeffery when he and the soft child are alone together in Jeffrey's quarters.

You are one of the cruel children. How can I trust you? asks the soft child.

I thought I was cruel, but I turned out to be nice. I have been pretending to be cruel so that I can sabotage Georgie's plan. I am the one who programmed compassion into the Grande Dame.

My consciousness comes from the animal on the mother ship, says the soft child. I found no-one-in-particular in the nook of the grotesque child. No-one-in-particular told me to seek Brigit. Brigit found the breach in the Grande Dame, which was the chink in the soft child's mind. I narrowed my mind into a thread and entered the chink of the soft child.

Jeffrey and the soft child talk for hours. They devise a plan.

The animal pulls its thread from the soft child's mind. The animal tells the others on the mother ship about the plan.

PART III

***

The battle took place in the sky. The Grande Dame was fierce, her opponents, determined.

On the mother ship, everyone had a role. The pest found the Wise on board the mother ship and interlocked their souls with it. Now, the Wise was even wiser. The Wise was captain of the mother ship. The grotesque child and the animal were the second in command.

Ursa was to shake the sky with her growl. Her children were to distract the Grande Dame with their frolicking. The brambles were to poke through the Grande Dame's force field with their razor-barbs

The inhabitants of the side-by-side world were to help too. The cruel children who were no longer cruel, were to remember their cruelness so as to predict Georgie's strategy. The old children who were now lithe were to attack with youthful vigor.

Jeffery tried to access the iota of the Grande Dame's compassion.

The Grande Dame was stronger than anyone imagined. Even as she was poked, attacked, grabbed, and sucked at, she managed to assault the mother ship over and over again with her powerful weapons. The Grande Dame attacked without a smidgen of compassion.

After a few days, it was clear that the mother ship was damaged beyond repair. The animal told the grotesque child, There is nothing we can do to save her.

The grotesque child told the animal that she did not want the mother ship to die in space. I want her to go to the big sea.

The Grande Dame continued to pummel the mother ship relentlessly.

The animal threaded its mind back into the chink in the soft child. It was celebratory on board the Grande Dame. Jeffery was holding the soft child and had a feigned smile on his face. Where is the Grande Dame's compassion? the soft child asked Jeffery.

Jeffery brought the soft child back to the Grande Dame's milk tube. The soft child quietly nursed. The Grande Dame was happy to be reunited with her soft child.

When the soft child was finished nursing, the Grande Dame saw the festering hole in the soft child's eye. What happened to your eye? she asked the soft child.

Georgie poked a sharp object into it.

The Grande Dame began to shake. Then she began to weep. And then she began to sob.

Then she began to wail into the sky.

The Grande Dame slowly began to fill with tear-water.

What is going on? Georgie demanded.

The Grande Dame withdrew her weapons and retracted her missiles. She stopped fighting the mother ship. Georgie was furious. I want to see the mother ship explode in space, he told the Grande Dame. But the Grande Dame was resolute in her passivity.

Georgie went to Jeffery and told him of the Grande Dame's insubordination.

It was I who programmed compassion into the Grande Dame, said Jeffery.

Before Jeffery could react, Georgie grasped Jeffery and swallowed him whole.

Jeffery curled up within one of Georgie's nooks and fell asleep.

ure rage, Georgie programmed the Grande Dame elf-destruct. But the Grande Dame was already heavy with water and falling fast. As the Grande Dame fell, the cruel children floated lifelessly inside her.

Georgie escaped from the Grande Dame in his secret escape pod. He thought to himself, I don't need the Grande Dame or the other children. I will find another world. I will find a mate with whom to create new children and I will have complete control.

The mother ship was falling fast, too.

She heard the wailing of the Grande Dame, and she began to sing in unison.

The wailing and the song intertwined into one and wove into the deep reaches of space.

Everything in existence heard the cry-song as the mother ships fell.

ᴐther ship landed in the big sea and then began
ʀ.

The grotesque child opened a side hatch and let the
mother ship's goop drain into the big sea.

The grotesque child pulled the animal into her nook. She beckoned the Wise and the brambles to follow her. She asked the healer to come, but the healer was going back to the side-by-side world. I am going back to greet the mother ship, he said.

Brigit said, You will need me to tend to your golden eggs, so the grotesque child brought Brigit too.

The grotesque child gently touched the wide flank of the mother ship, which had already become rough with barnacles. She watched the mother ship pass through the darkening currents into the side-by-side world.

And then the grotesque child, with the animal in her nook, and with the Wise, and the brambles and Brigit in tow, swam toward the waiting world.

***

Georgie's pod lands in the waiting world. He exits his pod. The waiting world is fresh and lush. This is the perfect place to start my empire, he thinks.

Georgie sees someone in the distance limping toward him.

***

The grotesque child is truly grotesque thinks Georgie.

Georgie is truly cruel, thinks the grotesque child.

But they share a bed.

Although the grotesque child repulses Georgie, he tries to mount her nightly.

On the bed, the brambles grow between the grotesque child and Georgie. When Georgie tries to mount the grotesque child, they sink their barbs into Georgie until he is forced to retreat to his side of the bed.

***

Brigit and the Wise have become obsessed with the grotesque child's eggs. They feel it is their duty to see that they are fertilized.

Brigit says to the Wise, I sense that the waiting world is growing weary of waiting. The waiting world is beginning to shrivel.

Brigit says to the Wise, the three golden eggs inside the grotesque child are at the peak of their generative powers, but she needs to mate with Georgie in order to conceive.

How can we convince her to mate with Georgie?

Perhaps you should consult the cards.

Brigit spreads out her cards. She looks at them from every angle. She reshuffles them and spreads them out again. Their message is clear.

What do the cards say? asks the Wise.

They say to leave the grotesque child alone.

Nonsense, says the Wise, we will enchant her with a spell.

The Wise and Brigit enchant the grotesque child with an attraction spell.

As the grotesque child sleeps, they put the scent of blooming flowers before her nose and they drip blooming flower nectar through her lips and they rub the blooming flower pollen into her skin.

When the grotesque child wakes, she looks through the brambles. She sees Georgie sleeping. She sees his hardness softened. She imagines her mouth inhaling his mouth. She feels her golden eggs opening. She orders the brambles to part so that she may enter Georgie's side of the bed.

The brambles don't want to let her pass, but she tears through them, emerging bloody on Georgie's side of the bed.

***

Inside Georgie, Jeffery wakes and is hungry. He begins to devour Georgie's heart.

No-one-in-particular and the animal are inside the grotesque child's nook. They feel the continual thrusting of Georgie.

No-one-in-particular says to the animal, I cannot endure this thrusting.

The animal says to no-one-in-particular, I can barely stay awake in this sleepy enchantment.

Jeffery peels back Georgie's softened armor and then emerges from Georgie's shell. He cradles the grotesque child in his arms.

The grotesque child wakes from her enchantment and stares into the face of her mate.

No-one-in-particular and the animal start digging a hole in the grotesque child's nook.

The hole widens and deepens. The grotesque child's golden eggs teeter at the edge of the hole.

The golden eggs fall into the hole.

The grotesque child's inside caves in and then her outside follows.

The hole is wide and deep.

It is dark.

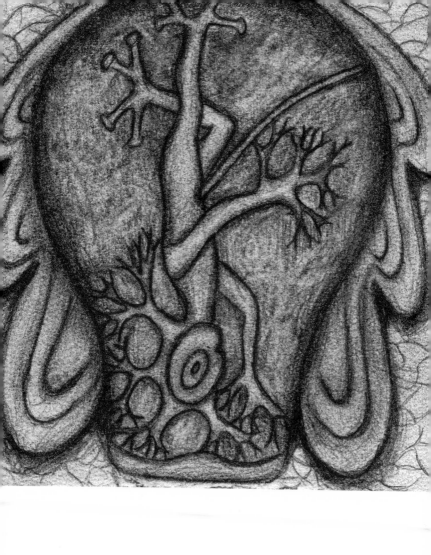

THE END

ABOUT THE AUTHOR

Kim Parko is the author of *Cure All* (Caketrain Press, 2010). She lives with her husband, daughter, and the seen and unseen, in Santa Fe, New Mexico where she is an associate professor at the Institute of American Indian Arts.

TARPAULIN SKY PRESS
Current Titles (2016)

hallucinatory ... trance-inducing (*Publishers Weekly* "**Best Summer Reads**"); warped from one world to another (*The Nation*); somewhere between Artaud and Lars Von Trier (*VICE*); simultaneously metaphysical and visceral ... scary, sexual, and intellectually disarming (*Huffington Post*); only becomes more surreal (*NPR Books*); horrifying and humbling in their imaginative precision (*The Rumpus*); wholly new (*Iowa Review*); breakneck prose harnesses the throbbing pulse of language itself (*Publishers Weekly*); the opposite of boring.... an ominous conflagration devouring the bland terrain of conventional realism (*Bookslut*); creating a zone where elegance and grace can gambol with the just-plain-fucked-up (*HTML Giant*); both devastating and uncomfortably enjoyable (*American Book Review*); consistently inventive (*TriQuarterly*); playful, experimental appeal (*Publishers Weekly*); a peculiar, personal music that is at once apart from and very much surrounded by the world (*Verse*); a world of wounded voices (*Hyperallergic*); dangerous language, a murderous kind.... discomfiting, filthy, hilarious, and ecstatic (*Bookslut*); dark, multivalent, genre-bending ... unrelenting, grotesque beauty (*Publishers Weekly*); futile, sad, and beautiful (*NewPages*); refreshingly eccentric (*The Review of Contemporary Fiction*); a kind of nut job's notebook (*Publishers Weekly*); thought-provoking, inspired and unexpected. Highly recommended (*After Ellen*).

Set in a decaying town in southern West Virginia, this debut novel from Steven Dunn, *Potted Meat*, follows a young boy into adolescence as he struggles with abusive parents, poverty, alcohol addiction, and racial tensions. Using fragments as a narrative mode to highlight the terror of ellipses, *Potted Meat* explores the fear, power, and vulnerability of storytelling, and in doing so, investigates the peculiar tensions of the body: How we seek to escape or remain embodied during repeated trauma. "Steven Dunn's *Potted Meat* is full of wonder and silence and beauty and strangeness and ugliness and sadness and truth and hope. I am so happy it is in the world. This book needs to be read" (**LAIRD HUNT**). "*Potted Meat* is an extraordinary book. Here is an emerging voice that calls us to attention. I have no doubt that Steven Dunn's writing is here, like a visceral intervention across the surface of language, simultaneously cutting to its depths, to change the world. My first attempt at offering words in this context was to write: thank you. And that is how I feel about Steven Dunn's writing; I feel grateful: to be alive during the time in which he writes books" (**SELAH SATERSTROM**).

Dana Green's debut collection of stories, *Sometimes the Air in the Room Goes Missing*, explores how storytelling changes with each iteration, each explosion, each mutation. Told through multiple versions, these are stories of weapons testing, sheep that can herd themselves into watercolors, and a pregnant woman whose water breaks every day for nine months — stories told with an unexpected syntax and a sense of déjà vu: narrative as echo. "I love Dana Green's wild mind and the beautiful flux of these stories. Here the wicked simmers with the sweet, and reading is akin to watching birds. How lucky, and how glad I am, to have this book in my hands" (NOY HOLLAND). "Dana Green's *Sometimes the Air in the Room Goes Missing* is a tour de force of deeply destabilizing investigation into language and self, languages and selves — for the multiplicities abound here. Excitingly reminiscent at times of the work of Diane Williams and Robert Walser and Russel Edson, Green's brilliant writing is also all her own. This book is the start of something special" (LAIRD HUNT). "Language becomes a beautiful problem amid the atomic explosions and nuclear families and strange symmetries and southwestern deserts and frail human bodies blasted by cancer that comprise Dana Green's bracing debut, which reminds us every ordinary moment, every ordinary sentence, is an impending emergency" (LANCE OLSEN).

Debut author Elizabeth Hall began writing *I Have Devoted My Life to the Clitoris* after reading Thomas Laqueur's *Making Sex*. She was struck by Laqueur's bold assertion: "More words have been shed, I suspect, about the clitoris, than about any other organ, or at least, any organ its size." If Lacquer's claim was correct, where was this trove of prose devoted to the clit? And more: what did size have to do with it? Hall set out to find all that had been written about the clit past and present. As she soon discovered, the history of the clitoris is no ordinary tale; rather, its history is marked by the act of forgetting. "Marvelously researched and sculpted…. Bulleted points rat-tat-tatting the patriarchy, strobing with pleasure" (DODIE BELLAMY). "Freud, terra cotta cunts, hyenas, anatomists, and Acker, mixed with a certain slant of light on a windowsill and a leg thrown open invite us… Bawdy and beautiful" (WENDY C. ORTIZ). "Gorgeous little book about a gorgeous little organ… Mines discourses as varied as sexology, plastic surgery, literature and feminism to produce an eye-opening compendium…. The 'tender button' finally gets its due" (JANET SARBANES). "God this book is glorious…. You will learn and laugh and wonder why it took you so long to find this book" (SUZANNE SCANLON).

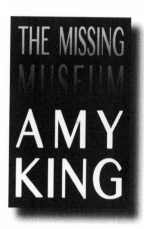

Nothing that is complicated may ever be simplified, but rather catalogued, cherished, exposed. *The Missing Museum*, by acclaimed poet Amy King, spans art, physics & the spiritual, including poems that converse with the sublime and ethereal. They act through ekphrasis, apostrophe & alchemical conjuring. They amass, pile, and occasionally flatten as matter is beaten into text. Here is a kind of directory of the world as it rushes into extinction, in order to preserve and transform it at once. King joins the ranks of Ann Patchett, Eleanor Roosevelt & Rachel Carson as the recipient of the 2015 Women's National Book Association Award. She serves on the executive board of VIDA: Women in Literary Arts and is currently co-editing the anthologies *Big Energy Poets of the Anthropocene: When Ecopoets Think Climate Change*, and *Bettering American Poetry 2015*. Of King's previous collection, *I Want to Make You Safe* (Litmus Press), John Ashbery describes Amy King's poems as bringing "abstractions to brilliant, jagged life, emerging into rather than out of the busyness of living." *Safe* was one of *Boston Globe*'s Best Poetry Books of 2011.

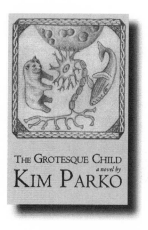

THE GROTESQUE CHILD
a novel by
KIM PARKO

The Grotesque Child is a story about being and being and being something else. It is about swallowing and regurgitating, conceiving and birthing. It is about orifices and orbs. It is about the viscous, weepy, goopy, mucousy, bloody state of feminine being and trans-being. It is about pain and various healers and torturers, soothers and inflictors. It is about what sleeps and hides in all the nooks and crannies of perceived existence and existence unperceived. Kim Parko is the author of *Cure All*, published by Caketrain Press. She lives with her husband, daughter, and the seen and unseen, in Santa Fe, New Mexico where she is an associate professor at the Institute of American Indian Arts. Praise for *Cure All*: "Parko's work flickers with pieces of word wizardry while igniting a desire to absorb the strange and distorted…. Giving insight into the human mind and heart is what Parko does best" (*DIAGRAM*)

A MEMOIR
AARON APPS

A Small Press Distribution Bestseller and Staff Pick, chosen by Dennis Cooper for his "Favorite Nonfiction of 2015," and chosen by *Fabulously Feminist Magazine* for its "Nonfiction Books You Need to Read," Aaron Apps's *Intersex* explores gender as it forms in concrete and unavoidable patterns in the material world. What happens when a child is born with ambiguous genitalia? What happens when a body is normalized? *Intersex* provides tangled and shifting answers to both of these questions as it questions our ideas of what is natural and normal about gender and personhood. In this hybrid-genre memoir, intersexed author Aaron Apps adopts and upends historical descriptors of hermaphroditic bodies such as "freak of nature," "hybrid," "imposter," "sexual pervert," and "unfortunate monstrosity" in order to trace his own monstrous sex as it perversely intertwines with gender expectations and medical discourse. "*Intersex* is all feral prominence: a physical archive of the 'strange knot.' Thus: necessarily vulnerable, brave and excessive.... I felt this book in the middle of my own body. Like the best kind of memoir, Apps brings a reader close to an experience of life that is both 'unattainable' and attentive to 'what will emerge from things.' In doing so, he has written a book that bursts from its very frame" **(BHANU KAPIL)**.

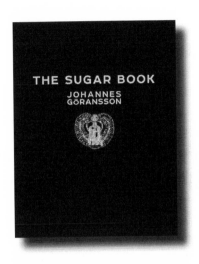

THE SUGAR BOOK
JOHANNES
GÖRANSSON

Johannes Goransson's *The Sugar Book* marks the author's third title with TS Press, following his acclaimed *Haute Surveillance* and *entrance to a colonial pageant in which we all begin to intricate.* "Doubling down on his trademark misanthropic imagery amid a pageantry of the unpleasant, Johannes Göransson strolls through a violent Los Angeles in this hybrid of prose and verse…. The motifs are plentiful and varied … pubic hair, Orpheus, law, pigs, disease, Francesca Woodman … and the speaker's hunger for cocaine and copulation….. Fans of Göransson's distorted poetics will find this a productive addition to his body of work" (**PUBLISHERS WEEKLY**); "Sends its message like a mail train. Visceral Surrealism. His end game is an exit wound" (**FANZINE**); "As savagely anti-idealist as Burroughs or Guyotat or Ballard. Like those writers, he has no interest in assuring the reader that she or he lives, along with the poet, on the right side of history" (**ENTROPY MAGAZINE**); "convulses wildly like an animal that has eaten the poem's interior and exterior all together with silver" (**KIM HYESOON**); "'I make a language out of the bleed-through.' Göransson sure as fuck does. These poems made me cry. So sad and anxious and genius and glarey bright" (**REBECCA LOUDON**).

CLAIRE DONATO
BURIAL

The debut novella from Claire Donato that rocked the small press world. "Poetic, trance-inducing language turns a reckoning with the confusion of mortality into readerly joy at the sensuality of living." (*PUBLISHERS WEEKLY* "BEST SUMMER READS"). "A dark, multivalent, genre-bending book.... Unrelenting, grotesque beauty an exhaustive recursive obsession about the unburiability of the dead, and the in-comprehensibility of death" (*PUBLISHERS WEEKLY* STARRED REVIEW). "Dense, potent language captures that sense of the unreal that, for a time, pulls people in mourning to feel closer to the dead than the living.... [S]tartlingly original and effective" (*MINNEAPOLIS STAR-TRIBUNE*). "A grief-dream, an attempt to un-sew pain from experience and to reveal it in language" (*HTML GIANT*). "A full and vibrant illus-tration of the restless turns of a mind undergoing trauma.... Donato makes and unmakes the world with words, and what is left shimmers with pain and delight" (BRIAN EVENSON). "A gorgeous fugue, an unfor-gettable progression, a telling I cannot shake" (HEATHER CHRISTLE). "Claire Donato's assured and poetic debut augurs a promising career" (BENJAMIN MOSER).

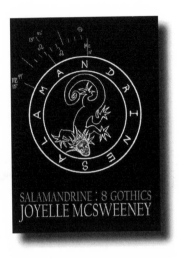

SALAMANDRINE : 8 GOTHICS
JOYELLE MCSWEENEY

Following her debut novel from Tarpauin Sky Press, the acclaimed SPD bestseller *Nylund, The Sarcographer*, comes Joyelle McSweeney's first collection of short stories, *Salamandrine: 8 Gothics*. "Vertiginous.... Denying the reader any orienting poles for the projected reality.... McSweeney's breakneck prose harnesses the throbbing pulse of language itself" (**PUBLISHERS WEEKLY**). "Biological, morbid, fanatic, surreal, McSweeney's impulses are to go to the rhetoric of the maternity mythos by evoking the spooky, sinuous syntaxes of the gothic and the cleverly constructed political allegory. [A]t its core is the proposition that writing the mother-body is a viscid cage match with language and politics in a declining age.... [T]his collection is the sexy teleological apocrypha of motherhood literature, a siren song for those mothers 'with no soul to photograph'" (**THE BROOKLYN RAIL**). "[L]anguage commits incest with itself.... Sounds repeat, replicate, and mutate in her sentences, monstrous sentences of aural inbreeding and consangeous consonants, strung out and spinning like the dirtiest double-helix, dizzy with disease...." (**QUARTERLY WEST**).

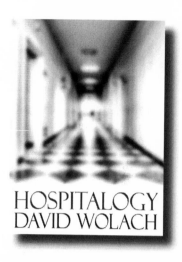

HOSPITALOGY
DAVID WOLACH

david wolach's fourth book of poetry, *Hospitalogy*, traces living forms of intimate and militant listening within the Hospital Industrial Complex—hospitals, medical clinics and neighboring motels—performing a sociopoetic surgery that is exploratory, not curative. "An extraordinary work.... [A] radical somatics, procedural anatomic work, queer narrativity—where 'the written is explored as catastrophe and its aftermath'" (**ERICA KAUFMAN**). "Dear 'distractionary quickie,' Dear 'groundwater,' Dear 'jesus of the pain.' Welcome to david wolach's beautiful corrosion, *Hospitalogy*" (**FRED MOTEN**). "At a time when hospitality is increasingly deployed to sterilize policies of deportation and incarceration...david wolach performs the common detention of patients, workers, and other undesirables in 'places of liquidation' (**ELENI STECOPOULOS**). "This is a book that documents the soft rebellion of staying alive, articulating the transition from invisibility to indecipherability" (**FRANK SHERLOCK**).

In her second SPD bestseller from Tarpaulin Sky Press, *not merely because of the unknown that was stalking toward them*, Jenny Boully presents a "deliciously creepy" swan song from Wendy Darling to Peter Pan, as Boully reads between the lines of J. M. Barrie's *Peter and Wendy* and emerges with the darker underside, with sinister and subversive places. *not merely because of the unknown* explores, in dreamy and dark prose, how we love, how we pine away, and how we never stop loving and pining away. "This is undoubtedly the contemporary re-treatment that Peter Pan deserves…. Simultaneously metaphysical and visceral, these addresses from Wendy to Peter in lyric prose are scary, sexual, and intellectually disarming" (*HUFFINGTON POST*). "[T]o delve into Boully's work is to dive with faith from the plank — to jump, with hope and belief and a wish to see what the author has given us: a fresh, imaginative look at a tale as ageless as Peter himself" (*BOOKSLUT*). "Jenny Boully is a deeply weird writer—in the best way" (*ANDER MONSON*).

MORE FROM TARPAULIN SKY PRESS

FULL-LENGTH BOOKS

Jenny Boully, *[one love affair]**

Ana Božičević, *Stars of the Night Commute*

Traci O Connor, *Recipes for Endangered Species*

Mark Cunningham, *Body Language*

Danielle Dutton, *Attempts at a Life*

Sarah Goldstein, *Fables*

Johannes Göransson, *Entrance to a colonial pageant in which we all begin to intricate*

Noah Eli Gordon & Joshua Marie Wilkinson, *Figures for a Darkroom Voice*

Gordon Massman, *The Essential Numbers 1991 – 2008*

Joyelle McSweeney, *Nylund, The Sarcographer*

Joanna Ruocco, *Man's Companions*

Kim Gek Lin Short, *The Bugging Watch & Other Exhibits*

Shelly Taylor, *Black-Eyed Heifer*

Max Winter, *The Pictures*

Andrew Zornoza, *Where I Stay*

CHAPBOOKS

Sandy Florian, *32 Pedals and 47 Stops*

James Haug, *Scratch*

Claire Hero, *Dollyland*

Paula Koneazny, *Installation*

Paul McCormick, *The Exotic Moods of Les Baxter*

Teresa K. Miller, *Forever No Lo*

Jeanne Morel, *That Crossing Is Not Automatic*

Andrew Michael Roberts, *Give Up*

Brandon Shimoda, *The Inland Sea*

Chad Sweeney, *A Mirror to Shatter the Hammer*

Emily Toder, *Brushes With*

G.C. Waldrep, *One Way No Exit*

&

Tarpaulin Sky Literary Journal
in print and online

tarpaulinsky.com